You Are B
Beautiful You Are

Written by LaToya D. Thomas
Illustrated by Arunodoy Ghosh Biswas

First paperback edition January 2019

ISBN 978-1-7336287-0-9 (paperback)

ISBN 978-1-7336287-7-8 (hardcover)

Polar Sky Publishing LLC

For Jadyn, who was the driving force behind this book- May all your dreams come true. You are beautiful inside and out! I love your generosity and your awesome sense of humor. Continue to be a star.

Love Love!

And for Jacques- May your imagination continue to lead you into wondrous places. You have a special gift of creativity. I see it in everything you do. Always follow your heart and let it lead the way.

La La Loo!

~Mommy

From your head to your tiny little toes,

you are beautiful.

Beautiful You Are! ❤

You, little darling,
are absolutely beautiful.

When you wake up in the morning and
you feel a little grumpy…

and when you reach up to the sky and
your belly peeks out of your shirt...

or when you try to do your best and you end up making a big mess...

YOU
ARE
Beautiful...

Beautiful You Are! ♥

You are amazing and unique, intelligent and sweet. You are funny. You're a star.

An individual. Yes, an individual you are!

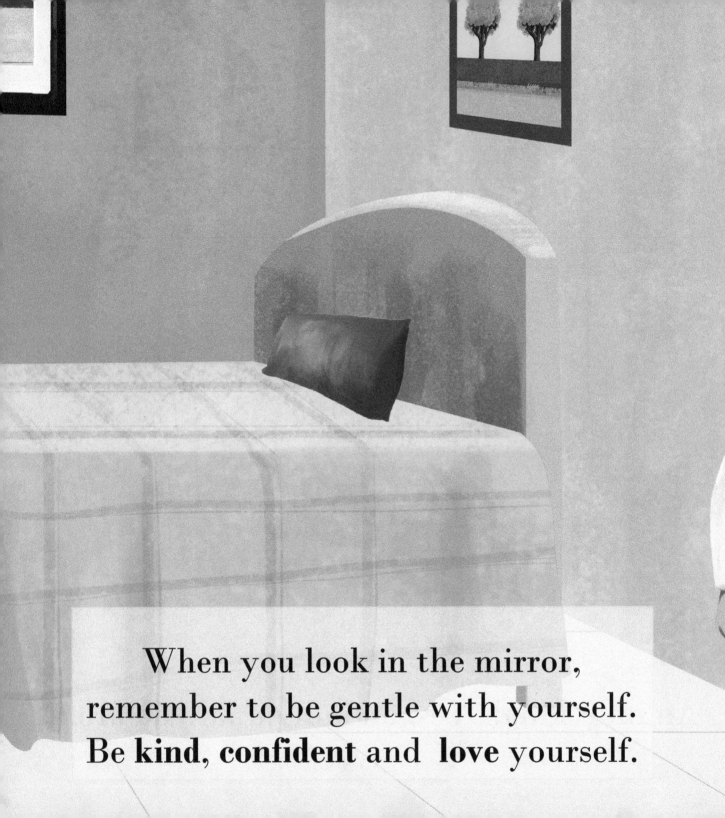

When you look in the mirror,
remember to be gentle with yourself.
Be **kind**, **confident** and **love** yourself.

Always remember…

YOU ARE Beautiful...

Beautiful You Are! ♥

Your eyes, your hair, your style...
Your skin, your fingers, your nose...
Your smile, your laugh, your shape...
even your thoughts, your actions
and your teeny tiny toes...

Each of these features make you who you are, and it's okay to be different.
You are a star!

You ARE beautiful...

Beautiful

You

Are! ♥

Always remember wherever you go,
however you feel and whoever you know...

...you are **brave** and you are **beautiful**.
You are **strong** and you should know.

You are a load of potential.
Carry it near and carry it far.

You are beauty. You are kindness.
You are a star. Yes, a star is who you are.

You ARE Beautiful...

Beautiful
You
Are! ♥

♥ **Seek and find** ♥

As you turned the pages of this book, you may have seen many hearts in the pictures. Let each heart be a reminder of the importance of self-love.

1. How many hearts did you see throughout this book?

2. Can you count the number of toys on each page?

3. How many books can you find throughout this book?

4. What is your favorite page?

5. Fill in the blank.
   "You are _____, beautiful you ____!

Great job!

Note to parents, caregivers and readers:

We live in a world where we are constantly judging others and being judged based on our looks, our size, our features and more. We often get caught up focusing on things that do not matter. Some of us lose sight of who we are in the process of living life. We even begin to judge ourselves, knit-picking at any minor imperfection and we forget how beautiful we are inside and out.

This book was written with the purpose of instilling self-love, a positive self-image, and acceptance at a young age in both females and males. Although I use the word beautiful, which many people may associate with females, I believe that males can also display beauty in many ways. I would like for this book to serve as a reminder that regardless of our imperfections, we are all unique and amazing individuals. In fact, it is our flaws that make us different from one another. They make us who we are! How beautiful would the world be if we accepted each other for who we are and also accepted ourselves?

Always remember that you are beautiful, beautiful you are! Please take a moment and share this message with others. After all, the more we love ourselves, the more able we are to love other people too.

-LaToya D. Thomas

For free activities and coloring pages,
visit latoyadthomas.com

About the Author

"I'm still working on my masterpiece…" Jessie J.

LaToya D. Thomas is a children's book author who was born and raised in Philadelphia, Pennsylvania. She currently lives in Montgomery County, PA with her three children. LaToya graduated from Bellevue University with a Bachelor's of Science Degree in Behavioral Science. She has also obtained an Associates Degree in Early Childhood Education.

For most of LaToya's adult life she has worked with children, so it was no surprise when she began a second career in writing children's literature. Her debut book, "You Are Beautiful, Beautiful You Are," is the first in a series titled, The Self Love and Encouragement Series. LaToya seeks to promote self-love, acceptance and positive self-talk.

When she isn't working or writing, LaToya can be found researching current events related to psychology, sociology and human services. For leisure, she mostly reads nonfiction books. LaToya loves swimming, shopping and creating vegetarian dishes.

In the future, she hopes to act as an inspiration to others, both through her books and in everyday life, and to volunteer in the community helping children and families in need.

www.latoyadthomas.com